Born in 1660, Daniel Defoe grew up in London. He wrote *Robinson Crusoe* in 1719. By the time he died in 1731, Defoe had written over five hundred books. Among them are two sequels to this story, in which Crusoe returns to the island as a missionary and converts those who were left behind. Some consider *Robinson Crusoe* to be the first great English novel.

When the stubborn young Crusoe ignores his father's advice and goes to sea, he pays a high price. For the next thirty years, he must learn how to live alone on a desert island.

Now Anne de Graaf, author of several children's books, has rewritten this dramatic adventure story, using simpler, more modern language. Here is one of the very earliest classics in a readable version for today's children.

To Erik

Robinson Crusoe

Text copyright © 1989 by Anne de Graaf and Scandinavia Publishing House

Illustrations copyright © 1989 by Francois Ruyer and Scandinavia Publishing House

Published by Crossway Books, a division of Good News Publishers, Wheaton, Illinois 60187.

First U.S. printing, 1990 / Printed in Hong Kong

Library of Congress Cataloging-in-Publication Data
De Graaf, Anne.
  Robinson Crusoe / retold by Anne de Graaf from Daniel Defoe's classic story : illustrated by Francois Ruyer.
    p.   cm.   — (Classics for children)
  Summary: As the sole survivor of a shipwreck, an Englishman lives for nearly thirty years on a deserted island.
  [1. Shipwrecks—Fiction. 2. Survival—Fiction.] I. Ruyer, François, ill. II. Defoe, Daniel, 1661?-1731.
Robinson Crusoe. III. Title. IV. Series: De Graaf, Anne. Classics for children.
PZ7.D33946Ro 1989   [Fic]—dc20   90-46733
ISBN 0-89107-601-8

99   98   97   96   95   94   93   92   91   90
15   14   13   12   11   10   9   8   7   6   5   4   3   2   1

Classics for Children

Robinson Crusoe

Retold by Anne de Graaf
from Daniel Defoe's classic story

Illustrated by Francois Ruyer

CROSSWAY BOOKS • WHEATON ILLINOIS
A DIVISION OF GOOD NEWS PUBLISHERS

Contents

CHAPTER 1
Father Knows Best

My name is Robinson Crusoe. I was born in England in the year 1632. Ever since I was very young, I had always wanted to go to sea and explore, but my father was against it. If I had taken his advice early on, it would have saved me much pain. But then I would not have had my strange and amazing adventure either.

I would beg him from the time I was just a boy, "Please, Father, please let me be a sailor!"

"No, my son. That is a foolish dream,

and someday you will realize it. I know it sounds exciting to sail away and see the world. But it would be much better for you to learn a trade. Become an honest businessman. You'll be much happier."

"No, Father, I just can't."

"You must. If you go away to sea, you will regret your mistake for the rest of your life. If you become a sailor, it will ruin you, my son. You will end up worse off than you could ever imagine."

I remember that my father reached out to hug me then. Tears ran down his face as he begged me to listen. "You would be all alone in the world. Sailors are rough men. Very likely, no one on board would care if you needed help."

My father's tears moved my heart. "All right, yes, I will do as you say," I promised.

But I was young, and after a few days I changed my mind. All I could think about was going to sea. So when a friend's father offered me a job on the ship where he was captain, I took it.

I could not bear to see how my news would hurt my parents. So I did not even say good-bye to them. I crept away at night and never saw my poor mother and father again. All they wanted was the best for me. If only I had listened. I wonder if my father knew just how true his words of warning were.

CHAPTER 2
My First Voyage

We had a good ship, and the captain was kind to me. He and the other twelve men had traveled far together, spending many years at sea. But no amount of experience could have helped us in the storm which hit as soon as we left port.

The wind howled. Great mountains of waves crashed down upon us. I stayed below, shivering in my hammock, back and forth, back and forth. My stomach turned inside out so many times I wondered how I could possibly still have anything left inside.

"Crunch!" The ship shook as the men tore down the main mast, hoping to keep the wind from blowing us over. But the gale just grew stronger.

"Oh Father, Father, you were right," I moaned. "I'm so scared! Maybe I'm going to die."

Suddenly, I heard the men shouting above the storm, "All hands, all hands to the pump!"

My friend poked his head in and yelled, "There's a leak down below. You may not be able to help with sailing the ship, but you can help man the pump!"

Below decks I lifted the pump up and down, pumping until my back felt as if it would break. When it was my turn to rest, I saw a strange sight. The captain, first mate, and a few of the other sailors

knelt in the water, all praying to be saved from the storm.

Until that moment I had thought this was a storm like any other. Now I knew we were really in danger. *I'm going to die*, I thought. *I had my chance, and now I will surely die!*

When the captain finished praying, he went above deck and shot off the cannons. The great "Boom!" could hardly be heard above the roaring wind. It was a signal to any other ship, a call for help.

Hours later I heard a sailor shout, "There's a boat coming. They're trying to save us but can't come alongside. We're going to break up any moment!"

Amazing as it may seem, a ship anchored nearby had seen our signal. They sent a little boat of brave men who finally did manage to throw us a line and strap their boat to ours. We threw ourselves at the storm's mercy. One by one, we slid down the ropes into the tiny boat. Giant waves tossed us back and forth.

But just as we managed to pull away, our ship began to break up. The little boat was so crowded we sat on top of each other. As the ship lay broken, leaning to one side, many of the men started thanking God. A few moments longer on board, and we all would have drowned.

CHAPTER 3
A Second Chance

Our boat safely reached the other ship without losing a man. All agreed, though, that it was the worst storm they had ever seen.

As soon as we could make it to land, the captain of the ship let us off in an English harbor. The people there called us heroes and gave us clothes and money so we could find our way back home again.

Once on land, my captain found where I was staying and came to visit. "Young Crusoe, I know you took this trip as a trial. If it went well, you would have made yourself into a sailor. But this storm is nothing less than a sign from God that you must never go to sea again. Tell me, what did your parents think about your going away?"

When I told him, the captain shook me by the shoulders. "And you came onto my ship after your father told you not to? You're no better than Jonah! No wonder such a terrible storm hit us! If you know what's good for you, you'll go straight back home and thank God for sparing your life. If you try to go to sea again, I promise you'll end up dead."

I was deeply shaken by the captain's words. Had it been a sign from God? Well, it didn't matter. I had learned my lesson. I would go home.

But it didn't take long for me to start asking myself, "What will the neighbors say? I'm so ashamed to face Mother and Father. Now what will I do?"

I didn't have the courage to go home. It's strange how most people find it harder to say they are sorry than to do the wrong thing. And yet it's the asking for forgiveness that makes a person wise.

It did not take me long to reach London. There I found a ship going to Brazil. I still had the money given to me after the wreck. So I paid my way this time. Just before we left, I heard that my father was trying to find out if I had survived that storm. But I was in too much of a hurry to send him a message. Before long I would pay the price for thinking only of myself.

CHAPTER 4
Shipwrecked

It was smooth sailing after we left the
harbor and headed out to sea. But
before long another storm blew up.
Believe it or not, this gale was even
worse than the first one.

On the first day, the wind blasted us
with such fury that we nearly went
under. For twelve days in a row, it
looked as if we would sink at any
minute. Great walls of water swept over
our ship from both sides at once.

We could do nothing but let the
wind take us where it wanted. At any
time, we expected the angry waves to
swallow us up. On the twelfth day, the
captain was able to get his bearings and
discovered we were very near the South
American coast.

The next morning the storm still
raged, although not quite as wild as
before. Suddenly, the ship seemed to
fall forward. At the same moment one
of the men shouted, "Land ho!"

Then someone else shouted, "We've
run aground! She's breaking up!"

We all ran for the smaller boat and
struggled to lower it over the side. The
rain blew in our faces, but we could see
that the shore was close. We all piled
into the boat. Could we make it to the
shore? It was our only hope, since the
ship seemed ready to break up any
second.

We were too scared of the storm to
even think about whether this was a
friendly place to land. Man-eating

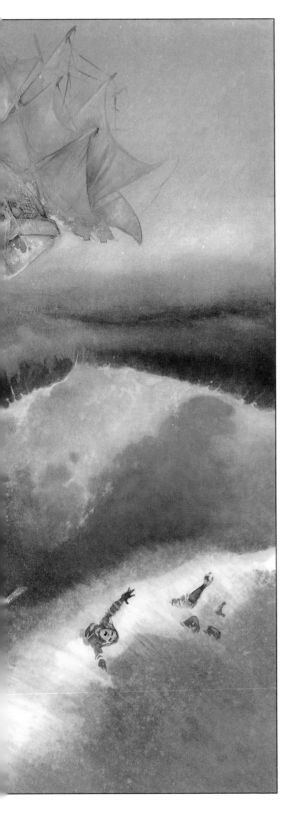

tribes lived on the South American shores. Who knew what awaited us?

But this was the least of our worries as the sea heaved up and down around us. We could see now, as we rowed closer to the beach that our boat would most likely be smashed into a thousand pieces by the force of the waves. There was no way out now. We pulled on the oars with all our strength.

All at once, a wave as tall as a mountain towered over us. We did not even have time to cry out, "Oh God!" before it crashed down, turning our boat over. I never saw the other men again, but was sucked under the wave. I stayed under water so long I thought my lungs would burst.

Finally I popped up to the surface where I gulped some air before another wave crashed down on top of me. That's when I felt sand scrape against my feet. I had reached the shore! I fell to my hands and knees, trying to crawl, but the waves kept pulling me back.

Then I saw my chance. Before another wave could snatch me away again, I scrambled forward until I reached dry sand. There I fell face down, and I think I must have fainted. The last thing I remember seeing before closing my eyes was an empty beach. There was no one in sight.

CHAPTER 5
Saving Supplies

I must have slept several hours because when I next opened my eyes, the wind had died and the sun shone out of blue skies. The storm was over. I can't describe how happy I was to be alive! It was easy enough to see I was the only man out of the entire crew who had not died in the storm.

As I walked up the beach, I lifted my hands to the sky and thanked God for saving me. Life seemed very special right then. The only traces I ever found of my friends were three hats, one cap, and two shoes. This made me feel all the more grateful to be alive.

I could also see that the ship had not broken up during the storm, after all. *Oh,* I thought, *we could have stayed on board and been safe! But look how far it is. How did I ever make it to shore?*

All these thoughts ran through my head that afternoon as I walked up and down the beach, looking for some signs of life. But there were none. What kind of place was I in? "Are there man-eating natives living nearby?" I whispered to myself.

That's when I stopped feeling so happy about being alive. There I was, without clothes or food. Wild beasts might eat me. And all I had was a knife! I had nothing to hunt with. How

would I eat? Soon it would be dark. Where would I sleep?

Now I felt as if I wanted to run away. But on a desert island there is nowhere to go.

With a heavy heart I climbed a nearby tree. I took a club with me in case a wild animal attacked me during the night. Then I tried to fall asleep in such a way that I would not fall out of the tree.

I woke up late the next morning. The tide was out and the beach looked so flat I could walk most of the way out to where the ship still lay. Once again I thought, *If only we had just stayed on board, they would be alive now as well.* Then I cried for my poor friends who were gone, all gone. The day before, I had become too caught up in my own problems. Now I was thankful again, just to be alive.

"I will make the best of this. I must," I told myself. I decided I had to try and get back onto the ship and save whatever I might be able to use. Who knew how long I might have to stay there?

So I stripped off my clothes and walked out to the water. Then I swam to the ship. I swam around and around it before I saw a rope hanging over the side. Hanging on to the rope, I managed to climb up. The ship lay on its side since the bottom had filled up with water. The next storm would tear it to pieces. I didn't know how much time I had, how many days it would be before

the weather changed again, so I set to work.

I went to the supply room and found most of the food still dry. Putting the flour and rum in a pile, I then tried to find a way to make a raft. I cut up some of the wood on the boat and strapped planks together. This was my raft.

I filled a chest with dried goat's meat, rice, barley, and wheat. Then I noticed the tide had changed, so I threw my raft overboard and carefully lowered the food onto it. Just before I left, I also found a bag of money and the carpenter's chest. These tools would be worth much more to me than the money in the months and years to come.

When I finally lowered myself onto the raft, I could see I would have a hard time keeping my chests and barrels from rolling off. As I came closer to the shore, the waves almost turned me over a few times, but I finally managed to drag the raft up the sand. "Now," I said to myself, "that's a good start anyway."

That night I slept in my tree again. I spent the next few days going back and forth between the ship. I brought back clothes and gunpowder, guns, hatchets, and more wood. Then, just when I thought I had emptied the ship of everything I might be able to use, another storm blew in. The next day the ship was gone, without a trace. I was on my own.

CHAPTER 6
My Island

Now that I had all my goods on shore, my next job was to find a safe place to store them. I had to find a home for myself, some kind of shelter from the rain and a place to hide, in case the man-eaters came hunting for me.

So I took my gun and hiked up a nearby hill. From the top I could see clearly that this was an island. There were two other islands nearby. My island had woods and sandy dunes. I saw no smoke or other signs of people. Nor did I see any wild beasts, except for rabbits and foxes.

As I walked back to the beach, I shot a great bird perched on a tree. I think it must have been the very first gun that had been fired there since the creation of the world. When I fired, birds of all different sorts and colors flew upwards like a huge rainbow cloud. The bird I shot, though, was no good for meat, so I left it in the woods.

When I arrived back at the beach, I was glad to see everything was just as I had left it. I still did not know if I was all alone on this island. Right then, it seemed my only company would be the ship's cat. I had found her on board and brought her back with me. She had stayed to guard my treasure of things saved from the ship. When I got back to the beach, I gave her some of the bread which had not yet gone stale.

For the next few days, I searched the area, looking for a good place to live. It was important that it be in a healthful place with fresh water nearby. I would need shelter from the heat of the sun, protection from men and beasts, and a view of the sea. If God did send a ship to rescue me, I might then be able to signal for help.

I finally found a flat meadow on the side of a hill which overlooked the beach. At the back of the meadow was a small cave. I made a half-circle around the area with strong stakes, so that it formed a sort of fence. Then I built a tent in front of the cave, using the sails from the ship.

I carried all my things up to the spot and set to work making my cave bigger. I was very thankful for the pick and shovel I had found on board. Slowly but surely, my cave took shape. No sooner had I put everything inside, though, than it rained, and the roof fell in!

I was lucky I wasn't inside when it happened. I thought to myself, *If I were to have an accident, there would be no one to help me.* And once again I felt just how alone I really was.

So I rebuilt my cave. It took me weeks to dig out the dirt and clean everything up. But this time I made sure the walls and ceiling were braced with planks of wood. I even put up shelves for all the tools and chests and guns I had.

Then I made a ladder by strapping together pieces of wood with leather strips. The stakes in the fence around my meadow soon began to sprout and grow as trees. So I used this ladder to get in and out of my castle, as I soon called this place, my strange home.

CHAPTER 7
Getting Started

It took me many months to get my home in shape. All that while I had to eat, of course. And the food from the ship soon ran out. So I often went on hunting trips.

Many different types of animals and birds lived on my island. The most useful to me, though, were the wild goats. On one of my first exploring trips, I saw them climbing the cliffs. I soon found that if I could climb higher than the goats, I could sneak up on them.

The first time I shot a goat, it was a mother with a kid. When I walked over to pick up the dead goat, her kid did not run away from me. Instead, he wanted me to pet him. The little goat followed me all the way back to my castle, and I lifted him over the fence. Besides the ship's cat, this was the first of many pets from my island.

This little goat gave me the idea of collecting a herd of goats. If I could tame them, I would have fresh milk and meat whenever I wanted.

Once I didn't have to worry about food and shelter, the loneliness of that place hit me. "There is no one here but me," I kept saying over and over. Finally the tears came. I couldn't help it. I was so alone!

"Why me?" I wondered. "Why do I have to be the one cast away on a desert island?" I felt very sorry for myself.

But then I heard the question asked a different way. "Why me? Why was I the one chosen to live? Where are the other men who climbed into that boat with me? Is it better to be here or where they are now?" I pointed at the sea and said out loud to myself, "Do you wish you were there?"

Then I remembered again how blessed I was to have gotten so many supplies out of the ship before it sank. Where would I be without those tools? What would I have done without my gun? And suddenly, I felt thankful again just to be alive enough to watch the waves.

From then on, whenever I felt I was being punished, I made a list of good things that had happened to me. I would say them over and over, like a song: "I'm alive; I'm not starving; I'm in a warm climate where I don't need much clothing; there are no wild beasts here; I have enough supplies, thanks to the ship, to help me live here all my life, if I need to."

As the days passed, I wanted some way of keeping track of my stay on the island. So I made a great cross and planted it on the beach. For every day I marked a notch in the wood. It did not take long for the notches to grow into rows. And then I had three and a half rows of a hundred each. I had spent one whole year on the island.

15

CHAPTER 8
A Way of Life

There were many things I had to learn how to do for the first time in my life. I had never been very good at making things out of wood, but now I became an expert.

When I wanted a table, I had to find a wide tree and cut it down. Then I spent weeks scraping away the wood on both sides until it became a flat board. That was my tabletop. I made the legs out of smaller tree trunks.

For clothing, I used animal skins. Whenever I killed an animal for food, I used my knife to help tear the hide off. Then I scraped the blood off and laid it out in the sun to dry. After this, I scraped the hide again and kept working with it until it became clean and soft. Then I sewed several hides together into a shirt or cape or hat or whatever I needed.

For candles, I saved the goat's fat and poured it into a small dish. Then I put a string in the fat and made a lamp. The light wasn't very steady, but at least then I didn't have to go to sleep when the sun set.

One day I walked to the place near the beach where I first stored the supplies after I took them off the ship. There I had one of my finest surprises. I saw small barley and wheat and corn plants growing under a tree.

"How can this be?" I wondered. These were no wild plants. "I could make bread!" I laughed. Yes, this was an exciting discovery all right, but how had it happened? Were these plants some gift straight out of heaven?

Then I thought I knew what had happened. And in their own way the plants were very much a miracle. Over a year ago, when I left the supplies under that tree, I had found a sack of spoiled grain. The mice had eaten most of it, so I threw it out. Some of those pieces of barley, corn, and wheat must have fallen on good soil. By pure chance they took root and grew.

"Was it pure chance?" I asked myself. "No. God has given this to me to show He still cares for me." The miracle of how those plants had grown in that place was just as great as the miracle that no birds had eaten them.

This touched my heart a little and brought tears to my eyes. Then I noticed there were even young rice plants growing nearby. "If I save every grain and plant them and save the next few harvests, soon I will have more than enough to make bread!" It had been more than half a year since I had finished the last of the ship's biscuits.

In fact, it was not until my fourth year on the island that I had enough grain to grind into flour and make bread. I lost almost all of my grain the first few times because I planted the seed at the wrong times of the year. Either the weather was too dry or too wet.

While I worked on my small crops, I kept digging my cave out deeper and making the wall around my castle stronger. Between the trees which now grew in the hedge, I piled stones. Now the only way in and out of my little meadow was with a ladder. And that I always pulled in after me so there was no way anything could attack me.

CHAPTER 9

More Surprises

I had tried my best to protect myself from wild beasts and wild men. But the very same day I finished my stone and tree wall, the ground shook so hard that I fell off my ladder.

"What is it? My wall! My cave!" I shouted. But there was no one to hear me. I was alone in the middle of an earthquake!

I could do nothing but watch as all my hard work fell down around me. The ground shook three times. Each shock brought more and more stones and dirt down into my cave and down from my wall!

When it was all over, a great rock fell down from the hill nearby. It made a terrible noise as it rolled down, down into the sea. Then I heard another terrible roaring. I ran up the hill and looked toward the sea. Huge waves came crashing onto the beach. The water reached clear up to the trees, higher than any tide. I could tell from where I stood that the shocks to the sea bottom must be even greater than what I had felt on the island.

I was so amazed, I could do nothing but stare in horror. I had only heard stories about such earthquakes. I sat down on the ground. "I'm so alone here!" I shouted at the wind.

It shouted back. In a few moments it whipped itself into a hurricane, and sheets of water poured down on top of me. I just couldn't bear the thought of going back to my castle and seeing all my hard work of the last few years ruined. But the rain forced me to find shelter.

When I reached my cave, I found that the damage was not so bad after all. Some outside rocks had caved in, but most of the inner room was still in

place. My tent had blown away, so I went into the cave to escape the rain. I sat shivering with cold or fear or both, I'm not sure.

Soon I noticed that the rain was coming down so hard, it would soon flood my cave. First an earthquake, then a flood! I had no choice but to get to work. I dug a ditch out of the cave so the water could run off. Before I knew it, I had forgotten to be afraid, and I no longer felt sorry for myself. I was just glad that the damage to my castle had been no worse.

The next day I started cleaning up. It took me several months to repair the wall. And I spent months cutting more boards so I could make the walls and ceiling of the cave stronger. Now there was no way it would fall in on me.

My days were filled with working on my home and looking for food. Whenever I wanted to catch fish, I strung some yarn together to make a long line. Even though I had no hooks, I still caught enough for myself. I dried the fish in the sun. Once I even caught a young dolphin.

The sea gave me many surprises. One day I found a large turtle, the first I had ever seen. Later I found out that the beaches on the other side of the island were full of them. But this first turtle gave me oil for my lamps, a delicious soup, and a large, waterproof bowl — its shell.

A few days after I found the turtle, the yearly rains began. I made the mistake of staying outside to finish fixing up the last of my stone wall. That chill plus the cold I caught after sitting in the rain during the earthquake must have made me weak.

I don't remember those few days which followed. I must have been very sick, but there was no one to care for me. When I could, I made sure a full jug of water stood nearby, and I tried to drink often from it. It is a terrible thing, being sick and knowing there is no one to help you.

I felt so scared. For the first time since I was caught in that terrible storm, I prayed to God. More than ever I felt the heaviness of my time on that island. If it was my kingdom, I was its prisoner. I had been there for six years already, with no sign of help coming from anywhere. God was my only hope.

CHAPTER 10
An Answer to Prayer

Later, when I checked the number of notches on my great cross, I found I did lose some days while I was sick. I had had such a high fever that I lost track of time and didn't even know where I was.

When I grew a little stronger, I remembered calling out to God for help. He had listened! Then I thought of when I had first arrived at the island. I had thanked God then for the gift of life.

The growing up of the corn had also been a miracle. But I had soon forgotten about that gift as well. Now I remembered my father's words for the first time in years. He had said that if I did take the foolish step of going to sea, there would be no one to help me.

"Father was right," I said out loud. "I didn't take his advice, and now I'm paying the price. I turned my back on good advice; now I have no one. I have no help, no comfort, no advice. Lord," I cried out, "please help me!" This was my first *real* prayer in many years.

In the days that followed, I saw my island through new eyes. God may have put me there, but He had also put on the island more than enough of whatever I needed. Then I thought again, *But why me, Lord?*

I knew the answer. I had not listened to my good father. I was lucky to still be alive! God had given me chance after chance to say I was sorry and start over again.

This thought amazed me. I went back to my castle and took out the Bible I had found in one of the ship's chests. The very first words I read were, "Call on Me in the day of trouble, and I will save you, and you will thank and worship Me."

At first I thought this meant that God would someday send a ship to save me. Then I realized how, in many ways, He had already saved me. This touched my heart very much. Right then and there I knelt down and thanked God for healing me of my sickness.

From then on, I made time to read the Bible every day. In the morning and at night I read as much as I wanted. Soon I found my heart deeply changed because of these good words. They also began to change my life. I saw so many things as gifts from God.

I said I was sorry for all the wrong things I had done. And I prayed that God would keep changing me and help me hope again. I am sure that God heard me.

CHAPTER 11
My Kingdom

I stopped seeing the island as a prison. It became my very own kingdom. And I was king over everything living there. So I thought it was time I went exploring. For all I knew, there might be treasures waiting on the other side for me.

So I set off with my gun and a pack of food. Beyond my hill was a long valley, followed by a wide plain covered with grass.

At the end of the second day, I came to some more woods. There I did find treasure. Melon plants! All around me were different types of juicy melons. It had been so long since I tasted some-

thing sweet, my mouth started to water just thinking about it.

While I traveled, I spent the nights in trees, much like I had during my early days on the island. In the mornings I ate melons and later, grapes. These grapes were another great treasure. Later on I brought sack loads of them back to my castle, laid them out in the sun, and dried them. Then I could eat raisins with every meal if I wanted.

This woods opened onto a lovely fresh meadow. A spring watered the plants around it, so it looked like a garden. As I walked into this little heaven, I couldn't help thinking I was like some English lord on his country farm. This was all mine for the having.

There were cocoa, orange, and lemon trees. I was surrounded by food! The place was so lovely, I thought, *Why not make it into a second home?* So on that trip I went no further, but stayed to build a shelter in that meadow between the trees.

Then I planted willow stakes around the meadow, as I had done with my seacoast house. These would later grow into a grove of trees. There was no opening so, as with my castle, I climbed over with a ladder, which I pulled in after me.

My "summer house," as I called this place, was just right for drying raisins and storing the fruit that grew nearby. I hung about two hundred bunches of grapes on poles, and then waited for them to dry. Just before the rainy season started again, I took them down.

I had learned that my island had two rainy seasons and two dry seasons per year. It never became very cold. But I knew I should stay inside during the rainy season if I didn't want to become sick again.

The four seasons also meant I was out collecting fruit, as well as planting my grain crop twice a year. I soon had quite a lot of dried food. But I had nothing to store it in!

CHAPTER 12
Baking Bread

During one rainy season, I had taught myself how to weave baskets. These were all right for some of the fruit and the ears of corn. But I still needed pots for the grain and for boiling water. And there was my old dream of baking bread. I needed cooking pots and an oven for that.

I never dreamed it could be so hard to bake a simple loaf of bread. "How can I do that here?" I asked myself over and over. The first problem was with the pots. I needed to find a clay which would not melt in the fire.

My first pots looked very strange and lumpy. After many trials I managed to make two large pots and several smaller ones. One day, after I had cooked some meat, I happened to notice a piece of clay glowing red in the fire. It had not cracked!

So then I tried putting my pots in a hot fire. I did not let the heat die, but fed the fire all night. In the morning I let it cool slowly. By that afternoon, my pots were hard as rock and glazed from the running sand. When I did the same with a large square pot, I had something I could bake in. Now I had my pans and an oven.

Next I needed a stone bowl and stick to use for mashing the grain into flour. I spent weeks looking for the right stone and finally gave up. Hard wood worked just as well. Grinding the grain also took time. When I finally had enough flour, I strained it through some sail to make it very fine. This I added to water and goat's milk, and soon I was baking rice and wheat cakes, as well as corn cakes. I never could make real bread since there was no yeast. But my cakes were the next best thing.

All these projects I worked on at both my houses, in between more exploring trips. When I finally did reach the other side of the island, I saw land far in the distance. I wasn't sure of where I was, but I thought that must be South America. I had heard about the man-eating tribes who lived there, so I was thankful to be on my island rather than the mainland.

On that far beach I also found hundreds of turtles and many different kinds of birds which rarely came to visit my side. Animals and birds seemed to be everywhere. As long as I did not fire my gun, they were almost tame.

On my way back from this trip, I caught a parrot by hitting it with a stick. I brought it home with me and named him Poll. With time I managed to teach Poll how to say my name. His was the first voice besides my own that I had heard on the island.

I often visited the other side of the island to hunt. There were so many more animals. I caught hare and fox, as well as the usual pigeon and goat.

Poll turned out to be a real friend. He stayed with me at both my houses.

CHAPTER 13
Another Voyage

Flowers surrounded my little summer home under the trees. Poll flew from one branch to another, calling, "Crusoe, where are you?" Between the parrot, my cat, and the goats, I had plenty of animals. I talked to them all, too, for there was no one else to listen.

I kept thinking about that far shore I had seen. If it were South America, then Spanish and Portuguese ships should pass by it. "Should I go there and run the risk of meeting those man-eating people?" I wondered. And even if I did manage to find land and a ship or a

settlement of Spaniards, what if they threw me in prison since I was English?

For weeks all I could think of was a way of escaping. Should I try to take a boat to the mainland or not? Finally, I knew my answer. I had been on the island for eight years now, and never once had any ships come by. I had to take a chance. If I did not at least try, I would never know.

So my mind made up, I came up with a plan. First I needed a boat. I looked around for a tree with a large, round trunk. With just my small hatchet, it took weeks to cut the great tree down. Then I trimmed off the branches and set to work hollowing it out.

I did all this in between my usual jobs of hunting, gathering food, and taking care of my two homes. I worked slowly since my tools were not the best for that job. After nearly a year, I had finished my boat. It was a fine canoe, large enough to hold all the supplies I wanted to take, large enough to hold twenty men, if it needed to.

There was only one problem, though. And I didn't think of it as a problem until it was too late. I had no way of moving the canoe down to the water! It was much too heavy for me. I could not even use a lever and heave the huge canoe onto the beach. So I dug a ditch, thinking I could somehow slide it into the water. But when I saw how much time it took to dig just a little way, I figured it would take me thirty years to dig a ditch long enough.

I didn't mind the work. Every day spent digging brought me that much closer to freedom, or so I thought. Finally, though, I saw that I had made two big mistakes. My boat was too large, and it lay too far from the water. After a year of hard work, all I could do was start over again.

Now, more than ever, I was sure I wanted to try and sail to the mainland. Surely I would find someone who could help me. It would be worth it just to see another human being. That's what I told myself.

But I had learned my lesson. This time when I chose a tree, it was much smaller. Once I cut it down, I knew it would hold two men at the most or enough supplies for a few days. I scraped off the branches, spent months hollowing it out, and then finally managed to roll it into the water.

After almost two years of work, I had a boat! Now that the moment had come, I felt torn. Here on my island I had been content. The world seemed very far away. There was no wickedness, no stealing or selfishness on my island. There was no waste, either. I stopped to think yet again about how I had everything I needed. In many ways, it was very close to heaven.

I sighed. "I still must go," I said out loud.

My plan was first to take the boat on a trip around the island. That way I could get my bearings and learn how to handle the boat. I would also still be within swimming distance of the shore,

From the tip of my pointed hat to my ankles, I was covered in goat's skins. I looked like some huge, walking goat. My jacket and shorts were made of goat's skins. The fur was on the outside, to keep off the rain. On top of it all, I had made a goatskin umbrella. This kept the sun from giving me headaches, as well as keeping the rain off.

I tied my big umbrella onto my canoe. This was my sail. Now I had a goatskin sailboat! When it came time to leave, I took a deep breath. "Here I go!"

When I set out on this voyage, I had no idea it would last as long as it did. I had been on the island for over ten years and still had never seen the eastern shore. I discovered that the island was much larger than I had thought. There was a great shelf of rocks which stuck out into the sea. Some of the rocks were above water, but most lay underwater. These rocks were very dangerous to me and my little boat. They caught me by surprise.

I steered far out to sea in order to go around the rocks. The farther I went from my island, the more uneasy I became. By noon I noticed my speed had suddenly picked up. I was caught in some sort of current. No matter which way I rowed, the current sucked me out farther and farther! There was no going back!

To make matters worse, the wind had died. The water carried my boat so fast I was afraid of turning over. When I tried to paddle out of the current, it hardly made a ripple. "Oh, I'm never

should anything go wrong. After that I would see if I could reach the mainland.

As I put my water and dried food into the boat, I caught sight of how I looked in the water. I was a strange sight. I laughed to think what anyone might say if they saw me.

going to get back!" I cried. And suddenly my safe home on the island seemed like a lost dream.

"What will I do? What can I do?" I knew the current must go far out to sea. Now I would die of hunger and thirst. What a terrible way to go!

A few hours later, I felt a little breeze on my face. I put up the sail and tried to steer toward the island. But I had gone so far away, I could barely see the island to tell which direction to go.

The breeze grew stronger. At the same time the current seemed to grow weaker. Then a strange thing happened. The wind pushed my canoe from one current into another. Now I was heading back toward the island as fast as I had moved away from it earlier. I was saved!

Together the wind and current brought me around to the northern side of the island. I steered straight for it and landed there late in the evening. When I finally reached shore, I fell on my knees and thanked God. Again, He had saved me. I brought my boat close to the shore where there was a little cove. Then I climbed a tree and fell fast asleep.

CHAPTER 14
A Footprint

When I woke up the next morning, I still felt very tired from my adventure. This part of the island, too, was rich with flowers and birds. I could hear birds flying above me in the trees.

The first thing I did was check on my boat, which was resting safely in the cove. "I don't dare try to reach my side of the island by sea," I said out loud. "What if the current should catch me again?"

So I decided I would hike back to my seaside castle. I ate a quick breakfast of raisins and fruit, took my gun and my umbrella out of the boat, and set off marching. It wasn't easy keeping track of the sun as I went down into one valley and up another. In fact, several times I became so turned around, I decided it would be better to go back to the beach and follow the shore around the island.

This trip took me nearly a month. I had plenty of food, but sometimes it took me several hours a day to find the nearest fresh water. For the most part, though, the trip was a good one. I felt more and more as if this island were my own special kingdom. I knew it so well.

But then I saw something that completely shattered the picture of my island as a safe, happy place. Around noon on a beach quite close to my own, I just happened to stumble on a mark

in the sand. It had been left by a man's foot, a human footprint!

"No! How can this be?" I cried out. So I was not alone after all! I looked around me, expecting to see a tribe of crazy man-eaters come charging out of the woods at any moment. But all I heard were the birds.

Then I searched for more prints. There were no others. Just this foot, five toes and a heel, imprinted on the sand, waiting for me. I had no idea who made it. When I put my own foot inside the print, I saw that this man's foot was much larger. "So he's bigger than I am," I sighed. This did not make me feel any better.

For the next two days I kept expecting every tree stump to jump up and attack me. My peace of mind was gone. I hurried the rest of the way to my castle. The joy of being back home after so long away was spoiled by this haunting fear.

I climbed over the tree wall, pulled my ladder in after me and relaxed for the first time since I had seen the footprint. I felt like a fox that had found a hole to hide in while the hounds pass him by. Nobody would ever find me in my castle.

I had lived on the island now for eleven years. In that time the trees around my home had grown into a small forest. Even though they protected me, I did not sleep well that night. I was too tired from the trip and too frightened by all that the footprint might mean.

I kept thinking, *What if they find my boat, or my crops, or my goats, or my summer house? They will come looking for me.* The "he" who belonged to the one footprint had quickly become "they" in my scared mind.

I must have finally dropped off to sleep, though. In the morning I woke up to the sound of a voice calling my name. "Robin Crusoe! Robin Crusoe, where are you?"

The voice called me over and over. I was so dead asleep that it took me several moments to realize I wasn't dream-ing. All at once I sat up. "The foot-print!" I gasped.

"Robin Crusoe! Robin Crusoe! Poor Robin Crusoe, where are you?"

The strange voice went on and on. No matter where I looked, I could not find where it came from. Then sud-denly, Poll swooped down and landed on my shoulder. He lay his bill close to my face and cried, "Robin Crusoe, where have you been? Where are you?" I was so relieved I almost cried.

I moved the bird onto my finger and stroked its bright belly. "Ah Poll, you don't know how much you frightened me." I realized then just how much my fear had taken over. My bird was so

happy to see me again, but I could not share his joy. This fear was everywhere. It even kept me from hoping in God. How quickly I forgot all the ways God had taken care of me during the past eleven years. All that remained was my fear of a footprint.

CHAPTER 15
Life Goes On

I had already built a strong wall around both my seaside and summer houses. Now I made up my mind to make my homes as safe as possible.

I did this in between all the other jobs I had to do. After being gone so long, I had more work than usual. Among these jobs was the making of more clay pots. I even tried making myself a pipe, thinking that if I took up smoking, it might calm me down a bit. Wild tobacco grew on another part of the island. Soon I was enjoying a smoke for the first time in nearly twelve years.

Not only that, but I managed to make a wheel, a potter's wheel. So instead of lumpy jugs, I could now make round, even jars. And I continued to make baskets of all shapes and sizes. These I used to bring home the meat I shot, or fruits and berries I found in the woods, or the ears of corn I picked in my fields.

I had by now great crops of wheat, barley, and rice. It took me some time to come up with a way of keeping the birds away from the corn when it was

ripe. I finally shot three birds and hung them up as scarecrows. That worked so well that few birds ever visited that part of the island again.

I used much of the corn to feed my herd of goats. After I saw the footprint, I moved my goats to a meadow almost completely hidden by a grove of trees. To these I added my own fence. Just fencing in the meadow took nearly a year to do. As with my two houses, I drove willow stakes all the way around the pasture. Then I filled in the spaces between the stakes with stones.

I had caught several goats and their kids. Now my herd was quite large. Most of the goats were tame. Whenever I entered the pasture, the little ones nuzzled me for the bits of corn I always carried in my pockets.

They were easy animals to tame. Whenever I brought a new goat inside, I tied it up close to the entrance first. Then I tamed it and when it was no longer afraid, I let it go free in the meadow. There was fresh water and plenty of shade there.

These goats were very precious to me. They provided fresh meat and milk. From the milk I made butter and cheese.

After I saw the footprint, the goats became even more important. I had decided not to shoot my gun so often. The sound might tell the owner of the footprint that I was here. I was deathly afraid that he might come looking for me then. So, thanks to having so many tame goats, I didn't have to shoot the gun. When hunting any of the other animals, I used a trap or snare.

In addition to all this, I was always gathering the wild grapes and hanging them out to dry. In the back of my cave I had made many heavy shelves. On these I stacked many pots filled with raisins. I had enough food to last me a lifetime!

As I did all my little jobs, my mind kept dreaming up different disasters which might happen, all because of that footprint. Where I had been so

happy before, now I pictured these man-eaters coming to my island by the hundreds.

They waited for me, watched me, to catch and eat me! One morning I lay in bed thinking this very thought, when suddenly I remembered something I had read in the Bible several years earlier. Before I saw the footprint, I had read my Bible twice a day.

Now these words came back to me, "Call on Me in the day of trouble, and I will save you, and you will thank and worship Me."

Like cool water on a fever, these words calmed me. It is hard to describe just how much comfort these words gave me. For the first time in nearly a year, I was able to relax.

I decided I would do the most I could to protect myself. But beyond that, I must trust in God. There was no other choice, except to be afraid all the time. And as I well knew, that was no way to live.

So I started building a second wall around the first ones that protected my two houses. I planted a double row of trees and made a path between them to the place where I could climb over the inside row of trees. Within a few years these stakes would grow into strong trees, just as the first row had. I left seven holes in my walls. Through these I put the seven guns I had taken from the ship. So now my walls looked like the sides of a ship, with cannons poking out. There was nothing more I could do to protect myself. The rest was up to God.

CHAPTER 16
Not Alone

Once my houses and goats were safe, I decided it was time to go back to get my little boat. If I could not bring it home, I would at least hide it to make sure no one else found it.

I never even reached the canoe.

I had followed the beach for part of the way, and then headed across land. I came back to a beach near my canoe, but it was at a place I had never been before. When I came down that last hill, I saw that finding one footprint was not so strange a thing, after all.

God's own angels must have kept me from this place before. Here I found many footprints, signs of a fire, and even worse, skulls and bones from human bodies!

"The man-eaters!" I gasped. It looked as if several canoes had landed. They must have brought prisoners with them. These poor people were killed, then roasted over the fire, and eaten!

I saw hands and feet, bones of all sizes. And the more I saw, instead of becoming afraid, I grew angry. "The savages!" I shouted.

From then on I made sure not to shoot my gun. I made myself a belt and carried one of the great swords I had found on the ship. I never went anywhere without this sword and my gun.

Dressed like some giant goat, and armed with a sword and gun, I knew I would be more likely to scare anyone I met. "No one is going to eat me!" I told myself. And I felt very brave and sure of myself.

I also took care not to build any more fires in the open. I didn't want the savages to see the smoke. So I found a nearby cave where I did most of my cooking.

Whenever I started to feel scared of these man-eating people, I just listed all the ways that God had protected me during my time on the island.

"Just imagine if instead of one footprint, I had come across twenty men that first time I was on that beach," I told myself. "If I have learned anything during these twenty years, I have learned to trust God to take care of me."

CHAPTER 17
One Friend

Another five years passed much the same as the twenty before them. Hard as it was to believe, I had spent more of my life on the island than off. It really had become my kingdom.

Every night I sat down to dinner and ate like a king. My pet goat and parrot stood nearby like two servants. I had two fine homes and fields of crops and lovely woods in which to hunt. No rich man in England lived better than I.

Thanks to my double rows of trees, no savage would ever find my homes. I was safe and healthy.

Then one morning, during my twenty-third year on the island, I saw them.

I was up early in the morning, just before dawn. I wanted to work in my cornfield before the sun grew too hot. Then I saw smoke coming from a nearby beach.

I stopped short, terribly surprised. Then I ran back to my castle, looking over my shoulder every step of the way. Once inside I loaded all my guns and put them in their places. Then I prayed to God to protect me from the savages.

I waited more than two hours and still nothing happened. I kept wondering what was going on down at the beach. So I sat a while longer, and then decided to risk spying on my visitors.

I left my castle and climbed the hill behind me. At the top I lay down on my stomach, pulled out my spyglass, and took a look.

I gasped again when I saw just how many there were. About thirty men sat around a large fire pit on the beach. Tied up on the ground near them lay two other men. Six large canoes had been pulled up onto the sand behind the prisoners.

"I can never fight so many at once," I said to myself. I prayed I wouldn't have to.

I could do nothing but watch then as the savages took one of the prisoners and beat him to death with wooden clubs. When they threw him onto the fire I had to look away.

When I looked back, I saw something very surprising. The other prisoner had been left unguarded while the savages worked over the first prisoner. Seeing his chance, he stumbled into the woods.

I was dreadfully afraid when I saw this. The poor man was running straight up my hill! It took a few minutes before the other savages looked up from their awful task and noticed he had escaped. To my relief they only sent three others to chase him.

Now it was my turn to move fast. I had already seen that this man who had managed to wiggle out of his ropes and get away could run as fast as the wind. "If he can keep it up for half an hour, he'll outrun them for sure," I told myself.

I ran down to the creek, halfway between my castle and the beach. I arrived there just in time to watch the

runaway swim across with great speed. *He is strong, as well as fast*, I thought. *If I rescue him, he may want to stay with me. Then I would not be alone anymore!* The thought warmed me all the way through.

I watched the three men cross the creek. One could not swim, so he went back to the beach. The other two took a long time crossing. I ran quickly up the hill so that I was ahead of the man running away.

Then I stepped out onto the path in front of him. The man stopped short. His eyes grew round with fright. He panted and looked behind him, then at me again. I think he was trying to decide which was worse, the men behind him or this strange bearded goat-thing standing before him.

I opened my hands upwards toward him, trying to show that I was friendly. The poor man looked as wild as some trapped animal. Then I showed with my hands that he should follow. He did, and I hid him behind a nearby bush. Then we waited for the other two.

They came stumbling through the brush, never dreaming they would soon be attacked. My friend and I jumped them from behind. I was careful not to shoot my gun in case the others on the beach heard. But with the end of the gun and some hard rocks, we managed to knock them both out.

I turned to the runaway and smiled at him. He smiled back. It was the first time anyone had smiled at me for over twenty-five years.

CHAPTER 18
Friday

My friend knelt to the ground in front of me and took my foot in his hands. Then he put my foot on his head. I think this was his way of saying he owed me for saving his life.

I would have reached down to help him up, but suddenly I saw the second man get up from the ground. He had recovered from the bump on the head we gave him. Now he stood with a bow and arrow pointed right at us.

I shouted at my friend and grabbed my gun. Taking aim, I shot and the savage with the bow and arrow fell face first onto the ground.

My friend had covered his ears like a child when he heard the blast. He ran away, stopped, looked at me, ran away a little further, then stopped again. The poor man did not know what to do. I

showed with my hands that he should come closer.

He came a little way, then stopped again. I could see he was trembling. Then he pointed at the gun and at the dead man. He wanted to know how I had killed the man without touching him.

Just then, the second man made a move. He must have been watching the whole time, but was too scared to do anything. Now he jumped up and ran back down the hill toward the beach.

I decided not to chase him. Instead, we climbed to the top of the hill to see what would happen. The man came dashing up to the other savages, waving his arms and then pointing and shouting. I think he was telling them about the gun. Instantly all thirty of the

CHAPTER 19
One Plus One

savages ran for their canoes. Leaving their half-eaten prisoner and the fire behind, they paddled furiously away.

I couldn't help smiling, thinking, *That will be the last we see of them for a while.*

Then I turned to my friend. He was watching me and no longer looked quite so afraid. Once again he knelt and put my foot on his head. He was a handsome and strong young man. When he smiled, he looked very gentle. I decided to call him "Friday" since that was the day of the week when he ran into my life.

I brought Friday back to my castle and gave him some raisins and dried goat's meat to eat. I made a little tent for him in the space between the two fences and showed him he should sleep there.

Then I climbed over the inside fence and brought the ladder with me. Friday was a prisoner on the other side. He could not run away, and he could not reach me in the night. I was safe and would not lose him.

I didn't have anything to worry about, though. Friday became the kindest, most faithful servant anyone ever had. He watched everything I did, and

him?" I asked. Of course Friday did not know what I meant. So I put on an angry frown and showed with my hands that it was very, very wrong to eat men's bodies.

After we buried the man, I took Friday back to the castle. I wanted to make sure he understood the lesson. I took one of my goats, and then pointed at the dried meat. I ate a piece of the meat and smiled.

"This meat is good," I said. I pretended to eat my arm, and then made a face. "But this meat is bad!" Friday nodded that he understood.

For the next few days, we climbed the hill and watched the sea. I wanted to make sure the other savages did not come back, but there was no sign of them. It was probably another blessing in disguise that I had fired my gun when I did. Now they would be afraid to bother us. I probably didn't need to fear being taken by surprise anymore.

Once I knew that, I took Friday with me back to the beach where he had been held prisoner. I had Friday pick up the skull and bones, which we burned. Then we covered the place with sand.

Once that was done, we could get back to the business of everyday living. I built a small hut near my castle for Friday to live in. I made him shorts and a shirt out of goat skins. I think these were Friday's first clothes, but he didn't seem to mind wearing them.

In fact, Friday didn't mind anything. No matter how dirty or hard the work

then offered to help. Soon he was able to do most of the work without any help from me.

After that first night, I showed him inside the second fence and let him explore my castle. I think the amount of food I had stored, together with the size of my cave surprised him.

That afternoon we went back to the body of the man I had shot. I showed Friday I wanted him to dig a hole. He nodded. But then when I did not build a fire for inside the hole, he looked confused.

"You thought we were going to eat

was that I asked him to do, he always did it with a smile. He never complained or grumbled. Of all the people to be stranded on a desert island with, Friday had to be one of the nicest.

He was a great help to me in many ways. Now that there were two of us, I had to have twice as much food. So together we worked in my fields. Together we gathered the grapes. Together we took care of the goats.

I taught Friday everything I had learned during my long stay on the island. I even taught him how to speak English. This was a great thing for me, to have someone to talk with. For so many years Poll the parrot had been my only friend who talked. After a while I got tired of hearing, "Robin Crusoe, where are you?"

Friday learned quickly. I showed him the secret of my guns. At first he was afraid to hold one. Then he kept wanting to look down the gun while I shot it. I think he wanted to see where the blast came from. But he soon learned that was not a safe thing to do. And after some time, he became quite a good shot.

The most important thing I taught Friday, though, was the idea that there is a God who cares for us. He was very willing to believe. In this way, as in others, Friday was as trusting as a child.

Soon I felt the happiest I had ever been during my time on the island. I had a friend. We had plenty of food. God had kept us safe from the savages. Every morning and evening I read the Bible to him and we both learned from it. There was nothing in the world that my man Friday and I needed.

CHAPTER 20
Friday's World

When Friday had learned to speak English better, I asked him how he had been taken prisoner.

"There was a battle, and my tribe took many prisoners. But my friend and I were apart from the rest of my tribe. The other tribe caught us."

"Why didn't your tribe rescue you?"

"They could not reach canoes in time."

"Well, Friday, what does your tribe do with the men they take prisoner?"

"We eat them, eat them all up."

"Where did you do that?" I asked Friday.

"Other side of this island. But now Friday not eat any more men. That would not make God happy. You taught me that," he said with one of his smiles.

I nodded, but was thinking of something else. As soon as the crops could be left for a few days, I told Friday to take me to the part of the island where he had been with his tribe.

It took several days. When we did reach the beach, I was shocked by what I saw. It was covered with pits and skulls and bones. Friday and his people had visited more than once, that was certain.

Friday and I set to work burying what was left of the bodies. I had explained to him that it was the only decent thing to do. Then I sat him down again and asked him about where he came from. I wanted to know how his people had managed to bring their canoes here without getting caught in the same terrible current that had caught my canoe.

"Friday, did you ever lose canoes to the sea?"

"No, never. We always leave from here at end of day. Water brings us back home."

I thought to myself, "He must mean he could catch the right current which went to the mainland from this very beach." Once again I started thinking about whether he and I might somehow escape my island.

"Friday, have you ever seen other men who look like I do, with white skin and beards?"

His answer surprised me. "Yes. Fifteen who live with my people."

From what Friday then told me, it sounded as if a Spanish ship had wrecked some years ago quite close by. Fifteen of her crew made it to the mainland. There Friday's people had taken care of them.

"You didn't eat them?"

He laughed. "No, we only eat our enemies. These men helpless. We take care of them after big storm."

So there were others besides myself! And now a plan started forming in my head. If I could get those men over here and keep them from attacking me, we might be able to work together and build a proper ship which we could sail to one of the Spanish ports nearby.

I thought of this plan all the way back to my castle. Just before we reached the castle, we climbed one very high hill. It was a clear day, and we could see for a long way. Friday pointed behind us and suddenly began to jump up and down with excitement.

"My nation! Look! My tribe's land!"

His face was so filled with joy, I thought, *He is homesick. Of course he would rather be with his own people than living as my servant.*

Friday danced and jumped, pointing at the fuzzy mainland that could just barely be seen above the sea. "Oh joy! Oh glad! There's my country, my nation!"

For several weeks after that, I thought about Friday and his people. If I let him go back, would he forget all about God? He might even come back and eat me as he had his other enemies!

No, Friday wouldn't hurt me, would he? I wasn't so sure. I finally decided that if I ever wanted to meet those ship-wrecked Spaniards, I would have to trust Friday.

A few days after this trip I asked Friday, "Do you want to go back to your home, Friday?"

His eyes shone as he answered, "Oh yes, much want to go home."

"Well then, I think you should go. But when you do, I want you to ask the leader of those other bearded men to come and visit me." Friday frowned.

"You're not coming?" he asked.

"No, I will stay here. But you go back to your family. I think that's where you belong." I could not forget how happily he had looked out at the mainland from that hilltop.

"No, I never leave you. Never!" Friday knelt to the ground and hugged me again. Now I began to cry as I thought of how afraid I had been that Friday would return with others and

hurt me. This man was so giving and unselfish. He really did love me and would probably even die for me if he had the chance.

"Oh Friday," I said pulling him to his feet. "All right, if you would rather stay, then we'll come up with another way to get that man over here." Now Friday smiled another one of his famous smiles. I truly had a friend for life.

CHAPTER 21
The Spaniard

I decided that if Friday knew which current to catch and when, there was no reason why we couldn't both pay a visit to his tribe. He promised that no one would hurt me. Now I believed him without doubt.

The boat I had made so many years before would be rotted by now. So together we set to work making a new canoe. It was easier to do when there were two of us. Friday knew much more about building canoes than I did.

A few months later we had finished a fine canoe. It was large enough to carry twenty men. This time I had made sure we built it on the sand. Even so, it took us two weeks just to move the canoe into the water. But once she was in, she was lovely to watch.

Friday was very good at paddling and turning her. I asked him, "Would this canoe make it to your land, Friday?"

"Oh yes, very fine canoe," he said.

I surprised Friday by putting a mast and sail on the canoe. When I taught him how it worked, he was very pleased that it saved so much work. Before long, he had become an expert sailor.

Now a feeling came over me that it would not be much longer before I left this island for good. I don't know if it had anything to do with finishing the boat. But I had been in that place for twenty-six years. "I will leave soon. I don't know how, but I will." I prayed to God about it and felt excited.

One day, Friday came running up to me, fear written all over his face. "Many canoes," he panted. "Many man-eaters!"

I let him catch his breath, and then asked, "How many? Are they the same tribe that brought you here?"

"Yes, same ones. But now there are three canoes. I saw them!"

He looked so frightened, I put my hands on his shoulders to calm him down. "Now listen, we have nothing to be afraid of. We have the guns, remember? And you can shoot as well as I. Now come, let's get the guns, and you can show me where these man-eaters are."

On the way up the hill I asked him, "Friday, will you be able to shoot them?"

"Yes, I shoot good."

From of the top of the hill I could see through the spyglass that there were twenty-one savages, three prisoners, and three large canoes. Some of the savages were dancing around the prisoners, while the rest were busy making a huge fire. I had seen it all before. It filled me with anger.

"Friday, we must stop them! Follow me."

We quietly made our way down the hill past the creek, until we reached the place where the woods stopped at the beach. From where we stood, I could see none of the savages. They were hidden by a clump of bushes.

"Friday," I whispered, "climb up this tree and tell me what you see."

When Friday came back, he told me all the savages were busy eating one of the men. The other two prisoners had been left in the sand, quite close to us.

We edged our way around to where we could see the prisoners. I gasped. One was a white man! *That could be me*, I thought. "Friday, we must save them."

He nodded and said, "That is the leader of the Spaniards I told you about."

Just the man I had wanted to see! I knew we had no time to lose. "Friday, you must watch what I do and do the same, all right?" He nodded.

I led him around the bushes so that we were within plain view of the savages by the fire. "Are you ready, Friday?" He nodded. "In the name of God!" I shouted as I fired into their circle. Friday did the same.

Because our guns were loaded with small shot, we wounded several at the same time. They ran, yelling and screaming, bleeding and in pain. I think we killed three during that first round.

"Now, Friday, follow me." We put down our guns and picked up two more. Then we ran as fast as we could toward the poor men tied up in the sand. For one of them we were already too late. But the white man lived.

"Friday, shoot at them as they run away!" I yelled.

He understood and shot after the fifteen savages who could still run. They had headed for two of their canoes and were trying to get them off the beach when Friday's bullets hit them.

Again they screamed and ran around in circles. They did not know what had hit them and were terrified. They paddled away from us as fast as they could.

"They won't bother you anymore," I said to the man at my feet.

He shook his head. "Senor," he said. I

quickly untied him and gave him one of my guns. There were still six of the natives hiding or wounded on the beach. So we three set about making sure none of them would ever reach home.

The Spaniard, who had seemed so weak when tied up, attacked like a madman. When the savages were all dead, Friday went over to the one canoe left behind. He yelled out in surprise. I came running over to see what he had found.

There, lying on the bottom of the canoe was a fourth prisoner. An old man stared up at us. Still frightened by the gunshots he had heard, he thought we had come to kill him. But when he saw Friday, he cried out joyfully.

"My father, my father!" Friday danced around the canoe. Then he climbed in and quickly untied the old man. Friday kissed him, hugged him, laughed, jumped around, danced, sang, then cried again.

It moved me deeply to watch this scene. I thought of my own father for the first time in years. "I will never see him again. He is certainly dead by now," I sighed.

Then I turned to the Spaniard. He motioned his great thanks to me and shook my hand over and over again. While Friday took care of his father, bringing him water and food, I did the same for the Spaniard.

We could not talk, but we motioned with our hands. He was

very thankful for the dried grapes and water I gave him. And when I pulled out my small bottle of rum, he smiled even more.

So now there were four of us in my little kingdom. My family had doubled in just one day!

CHAPTER 22
Preparing to Leave

Friday's father and the Spaniard were just too weak to travel up the hill. So Friday and I made a sling and carried them one by one up to the castle. They were both very surprised by the double walls and two homes inside.

Once Friday had settled his father, he came over to where I sat with the Spaniard. The two men knew each other. This was the leader of the group of fifteen who had been living with Friday's people.

Since the Spaniard had learned Friday's language, Friday was able to interpret for us. Yes, he said, Friday's people had taken them in and given them food.

"Ask him if he would like to join me in building a boat which could take us away from here," I said to Friday.

The Spaniard became very excited. "Yes," Friday answered for him. "He says he knows the other men would help. And for himself, he wants you to know he will follow whatever you say. The other men will do the same."

The man was so grateful to me for saving his life that he promised to help me in every way. That night I went to bed feeling closer to England than I had for years.

For the next few days the four of us talked about my plan. I asked Friday to ask his father if he thought the savages who had escaped would bring back more to hunt us down.

"Father says he heard them all cry out that you were spitting thunder. No, these man-eaters will not come back. They think you are some sort of goat monster."

I smiled at the idea. *Well*, I thought to myself, *that is one problem solved.*

Then I turned to the Spaniard again. "Why do you think your men would be willing to come here and work for me when they have not wanted to build a boat themselves?"

Speaking through Friday, he answered, "We have no tools."

"But do you have guns?" I asked.

"Guns yes, but no gun powder." That was a relief to me. Now I knew I had nothing to fear from the Spaniards. We could work well together as long as they could not hurt me.

"Do you think I can trust them not to attack me and take all this as their own?" I asked, waving at the castle and food I had stored up.

He answered honestly. "We have nothing over there, hardly any shelter. We are desperate to escape. I am sure my men will swear to follow your orders. I owe you my life. I will make sure of this," he promised.

Then the Spaniard had a very good idea. "Before my men come over here," he said, "we should make sure there will be enough food for them."

He was right, of course. I remembered that the children of Israel did not start grumbling when Moses led them away from Egypt until they ran out of food.

So once Friday's father and the Spaniard became stronger, the four of us set to work. The number of mouths I had to feed had doubled. But soon there would be fourteen more men living on my island. The first thing we did was clear more ground for crops.

Then we caught as many goats as we could and fenced in a second pasture. I was amazed to see how fast the work went, now that we had more hands. And we gathered grapes by the hundreds. We hung them on the tall poles which circled my summer home.

Months later, when one harvest had been stored and the second crop of the year planted, I thought we had enough food. It was time to send the Spaniard and Friday's father back to Friday's home.

CHAPTER 23
The English Ship

When the Spaniard left with Friday's father, they took two of our guns with them. Friday and I stayed on the shore and waved until they were out of sight. Both of us felt happy. Friday knew he would see his father again in just a little over two weeks. I felt sure I would be going home this year sometime. It had been twenty-seven years since I had first landed on the island!

We had given them enough food to last three weeks. But the actual trip should have lasted only four days. That's how long it would take them to reach the beach where Friday's tribe lived.

After eight days we started watching for their return with the other Spaniards. So for that reason I was not surprised when Friday woke me up one morning, calling, "They are come! They are come!"

Without even taking my gun with me, I made my way through the two rows of trees and ran after Friday. When I reached the hill I looked toward the sea . . . and was never more surprised in my life.

There, anchored a short ways from the shore, was a ship. An English ship! I could not believe my eyes!

Even as we watched, a small boat was lowered over the ship's side. "These are not the people we've been waiting for, Friday. Run back to the castle and get our guns." He looked at me with big eyes and nodded. Then he ran off as fast as one of the wild goats.

I cannot put into words how strange I felt. Great joy filled me at seeing a ship from my home country. "Surely these are friends," I told myself. But doubts remained. I had a feeling I should be very careful.

So instead of running down to the beach to greet these men from my home so far away, I waited for Friday to bring our guns. Then together we waited and watched. Before long, I saw I had made the right choice.

When the small boat landed on the beach, I counted eleven men. Three of the men walked in front of the others, with their hands held high in the air. Then one of these men fell to his knees and started begging the others.

As Friday and I watched, one man with a gun shot this poor prisoner even as he begged.

"You see," Friday whispered. "Englishman kill and eat other men, too."

"No, Friday. They may kill each other, but they won't eat them, you can be sure of that." I had seen enough, though, and motioned to my friend that it was time to make a move.

Slowly and quietly we made our way down the hill. We took the same path as when we rescued the Spaniard and Friday's father. Luckily the two prisoners were quite close to the clump of bushes where the woods ended at the beach. So we headed for them.

Then we waited until the prisoners were left unguarded. This did not take long since the other sailors were busy walking around the beach, looking for food and drinking the rum they had brought with them. Because the tide had changed, they knew they would have to wait until evening to catch the high tide back out to the ship. They

had tied up the prisoners and left them under a tree.

Once most of the sailors were at the other end of the beach getting drunk, Friday and I crept toward the two men. I know I must have looked very strange. I wore my goatskin coat and tall, pointed cap. I carried the guns Friday had brought me, as well as a sword, which hung by my side.

"Gentlemen," I whispered. The two

turned, looked at me, and almost yelled in fright. "Please, gentlemen," I said softly. "Don't be surprised by me. You have a friend when you thought you were alone."

"He must be an angel," the one man said to the other.

"Yes," I replied, "all help comes from heaven. But I can say for sure that I am no angel. Now quickly, before the others come back. Why are you here? I was watching when you landed and saw them kill that third man over there. Tell me what is happening."

As one of the men answered, tears of fear ran down his face. "Am I talking to a god or a man?" The poor thing was trembling.

I said again, "You can be sure I'm no god. If I were, I would be better dressed. Now please, don't be afraid. Tell me quickly, how can we help you?"

Then the other man spoke. "Our story is a long one, sir. But in short, I was captain of the ship you see out there. This is my first mate, and that poor man you saw them shoot was a passenger. Our crew mutinied and took us prisoner a month ago. Now they have brought us here to kill us. Can you really help?"

I saw my chance to be rescued. "Yes, of course we will help you," I said. "But tell me, how many guns do they have?"

The captain thought for a moment, and then said, "I saw them take only two. And one was left in the boat. Our hands are tied and there are eight of them, so they didn't think they would have any problems."

"Well, they were wrong," I said. "Now tell me one more thing. Should I kill them all, or are there some worth saving?"

Again the captain nodded. "Yes, all but two were good men. If it weren't for the two troublemakers, I think the rest would be a faithful crew. If you can save them, I'm sure they would help on the trip back."

This brought me to what I had really wanted to ask the captain. "If I help you—" I started to say.

But he finished for me. "If we get out of this alive, yes, of course. My ship is yours, and I will take you wherever you wish to go." The words were like music to my ears.

CHAPTER 24
Taking the Ship

Friday and I set to work. We untied the men and gave them guns. The four of us crept up on the others. Most of them lay sleeping in the sand. They had all had too much to drink. Taking them by surprise, we shot the two men the captain pointed out to us. We took away their guns. Then I sent Friday with the first mate to lock up the others in the area between my two rows of trees.

Next we had to find a way of capturing the ship itself. We decided to wait until they sent a second boat to look for the first. It would be easier to fight them on the shore. "Besides, I think if we frighten them into thinking you have an army here, they will give up easily enough now that the troublemakers are dead."

So while we waited for evening, the captain and I told each other our stories. It was wonderful to hear someone speak my language. He was amazed by my story. After all, I had lived on the island for almost thirty years!

When I had finished, the captain shook his head. Tears ran down his cheeks. "I can't help thinking that you were kept alive here by God so you could rescue me and save my life. Thank God you saw us!"

"Ah, my friend," I answered, "it is you who have come to rescue me." Just then I saw the second boat leave the ship. "Here they come. Follow me to my castle. I have a plan. But we need some of the prisoners to help us. Do you think they will?"

"Oh they will when I tell them the governor of this island will kill them if they don't," the captain chuckled.

When he saw my grove of trees and followed the winding path which led to the space between my two tree walls, the captain was amazed. He spoke to three of the prisoners, and they quickly agreed to do whatever they were told. Anything was better than dying.

When I showed the captain my home inside the trees, he shook his head in wonder. "You have done so much here," he said as he walked by the shelves of stored food and goatskins.

"Thirty years is a long time," I sighed. After a few moments I added, "Come, now we will get back your ship for you."

So we took the prisoners and told them our plan. When we returned to the beach, we found that another eleven men had come on shore to look for the first group. "That means there are just three left on the ship," the captain whispered to me.

We sent the three prisoners off to the woods, guarded by Friday. Soon they started calling for their friends, just as

we had told them to. While the second group chased these voices, the captain and I broke the bottom of the second boat by dropping rocks through it. We hid the first boat where the sailors would never find it.

When the sailors came back and discovered their boat was ruined, they started mumbling about ghosts. "It's a haunted island, I tell you," one said. "Why else would we hear the voices, but not be able to find them?"

Why else, except that Friday knew all the right places to have the others call from, but not be found. Our plan was working. The men broke into two groups to search the beach to find out why their boat had been ruined.

Together with Friday, the captain, first mate, and our two prisoners who had sworn to help us, we surprised first one group and then the other. We told them there was an army waiting to hang them in the woods. They believed us and followed Friday easily enough as he led them back to my castle.

"And now for the ship," the captain said. "It should not be so difficult. I know the three who are left on board. They will believe me when they see I'm free and none of the others are around." So the captain agreed to shoot his gun three

times once the ship was back in his hands.

While the captain took the first boat back to his ship, I climbed the hill behind my castle to wait for the signal. I knew Friday and the first mate could handle the prisoners. After all, we had an army somewhere in the woods to help us, didn't we?

CHAPTER 25
My Rescue

I did not want to fall asleep that night. I stayed up until nearly dawn, thinking this might be one of my last nights on my island. But I must have finally fallen asleep because the next thing I knew, I heard someone calling, "Governor, Governor!"

Then the captain was beside me. "Didn't you hear the shot? The ship is ours! They handed it over as soon as I waved your guns at them. They knew I must have had help or I would never have broken free. Besides, these men know we could easily hang them for the mutiny. They were only too happy to help."

I had been staring at the captain while he spoke. I hadn't really heard much more beyond, "The ship is ours!"

"Can it be?" I mumbled. "Am I really to leave this place finally?"

The captain saw my excitement, my great joy. He gave me a small bottle of rum. But no matter how hard I tried, I could not tell him all I felt at that moment. It seemed God had used us both to rescue each other.

Joy flooded my heart. "God does have a plan for our lives," I finally managed to say.

"Yes, my friend," the good captain answered. "He does indeed." Then we hugged each other and tears streamed down our cheeks. It was a special moment for us both.

The captain showed me the new clothes and boots he had brought with him. "Don't you think it's time the governor of this island showed himself to the prisoners?" We both laughed at the joke.

Putting on those new linen clothes was just the beginning of several new feelings I was soon to enjoy. That afternoon I walked to the castle and presented myself to the prisoners.

The captain had warned me that most were good men who had just made the mistake of listening to the wrong men. So I told them they could return with us to England, but that the captain thought they should be hanged there.

The men begged me to convince the captain to save their lives. I said I would try. In this way the crew were more than willing to come back on board the ship and do what they were told.

We did leave five of the worst men on the island. Before leaving, I explained about my homes and how they could live quite easily on all I had left behind.

I also left a message for the

Spaniards, promising to come back for them in a year's time.

Friday would not go home when I gave him the chance. He said he wanted to stay near me, no matter where I went. So after a long voyage, he set foot together with me, back on my homeland, England. I had been gone more than thirty years. I thank God for every one of them.